The Adventures of the Itty Bitty Bunny

Kimberly P. Johnson
Illustrated by Landa Smith

Pentland Press, Inc.
England • USA • Scotland

Other works by the author:
The Adventures of the Itty Bitty Frog

PUBLISHED BY PENTLAND PRESS, INC.
5122 Bur Oak Circle, Raleigh, North Carolina 27612
United States of America
919-782-0281

ISBN 1-57197-155-6
Library of Congress Catalog Card Number 99-070093

Printed in China

Nancy Haley
Kindergarten Teacher,
Cliffdale Elementary
Fayetteville, North Carolina

Kim Johnson succeeds in teaching children the valuable moral lessons of kindness, sharing, and friendship by introducing these character traits. She uses delightful animal characters which appeal naturally to children. A caring bunny, a helpful beetle, and a wise old owl cooperatively build self-esteem in the mean old otter, which ultimately brings a smile to his features.

This exciting story, with endearing illustrations, is an excellent choice for shared reading. It also provides an educational experience to unite children with their family and peers. Teachers and parents alike will reap the benefits of this character building tool for years to come.

Having read Kim's first book, The Adventures of the Itty Bitty Frog, in which the theme was kindness, I was thrilled to read this book! In The Adventures of the Itty Bitty Bunny, not only is kindness shown, but so is the true meaning of friendship.

Young children can certainly learn about caring and friendship from this story. The illustrations are absolutely delightful and make the book even more enjoyable.

Patricia DeLapa
Assistant Professor of Education
Methodist College

Priscilla Manarino-Leggett, Ph.D.
Department of Elementary Education
School of Education
Fayetteville State University

This is a wonderfully rhythmic and beautifully illustrated tale of the Itty Bitty Bunny and his success at making his friend, Otis Otter, smile. The value of using teamwork and being kind is exemplified in this captivating story. This book is a "must" for primary teachers and will certainly entertain young children for many years to come.

This book is dedicated to my niece, Whitney, and my nephews: Richie, Sean, Jacob, Vincent, Lamont and Lucas—I love you all!!

To Jeff—Thanks again for your wonderful support.

To Nancy Haley and Dr. Mary Anne Martin-Howell—Thank You!

To Aunt Shug—I love you and I'll miss you forever.
You were very important to my life.

I can do all things
through Christ
which strengthens me.

—Phil. 4:13

The itty bitty bunny was just hopping by the water,
when he ran into Otis, who was a mean old otter.

Otis had dirty brown hair that he did not like to clean,
and he always wore a frown because he liked being mean!

"Hi," said the bunny,
"Would you like to play?"

"No!" shouted Otis, "Just get out of my way!"

"That is not a nice thing to say," the itty bitty bunny said.
"Who cares?" said the otter, "And you are standing on my bed!"

3

"Oh, I'm sorry, I did not mean to.
You seem so sad. Is there anything I can do?"

"No!" said the mean old otter, with a sneer,
"I do not need anything, so just get out of here."

4

As the itty bitty bunny started to go away,
he turned and yelled, "Have a nice day!"

Otis just grunted at the kindness that he had seen,
as he sat on his log and continued to be mean!

The bunny wanted to think of a way to make the otter smile,
so he gathered up some leaves and sat down on the pile.

"Ouch!" came a voice that was filled with fear.
"You're squishing me. You're squishing me. Let me out of here!"

The bunny jumped up and dug to the ground.
It was his friend, Betty Beetle, making that sound!

"Sorry, Betty Beetle, I did not see you down there."

"It's okay, Mr. Bunny, but you gave me quite a scare!"

"What are you doing here," Betty asked, "down by the water?"
The bunny said, "Trying to make friends with the mean old otter."

"Good luck," said Betty Beetle, "Otis does not like to feel needed.
Believe me, Mr. Bunny, other animals have pleaded!"

"We have all tried to play with him, but he just does not care!
Otis is never friendly and he never wants to share."

"That otter stays by himself every day and night,
and when he sees someone coming, he dives out of sight."

"If I could only come up with a plan.
Betty Beetle, I would like for you to help me if you can."

"Let's see if Ollie Owl knows of a way
to bring a smile to an otter who does not like to play."

"Oh, yes," said Ollie Owl, "I know a wonderful way.
You should give him a party—today is his birthday."

"What a great idea!" said the itty bitty bunny with cheer.
"Come on, Betty Beetle, let's get out of here!"

So they began planning for a splendid birthday bash.
They had to hurry and they had to dash.

They put up a banner that was tied to the trees,
"IT'S THE OTTER'S BIRTHDAY! ATTEND, WON'T YOU, PLEASE?"

Susie Squirrel said, "Yes," and made her famous nut pies and the chipmunks showed up wearing their ties.

The animals took all the goodies down to the water.
"Happy Birthday, Happy Birthday to you, Mr. Otter."

16

Otis wiggled his nose and said with a pout,
"What in the world is this all about?"

"No one knows it is my birthday. If they did, they would not care.
I do not have friends in the forest. I do not have friends anywhere!"

"We are your friends," said the bunny, "and you are very special, too."
"Yes," said Ollie Owl, "so can we get a smile out of you?"

"Why should I smile? I never have fun.
Some animals tease me, they judge me and then they run.

"They say that I am different and that I do not have friends.
No matter what I do, the teasing never ends."

"Just because others are mean to you is no reason to be mean back. If you start to be kind, maybe they will get on the right track!"

The otter said, "Well, I have not smiled in a while, but I will try."
So he did and his frown reached up to the sky.

"Hooray!" yelled the animals, "Otis is no longer mean.
He smiled for us all the biggest smile we have ever seen."

22

Once again the itty bitty bunny had done a good deed for the day,
so then he sat and watched the otter jump into the water to play.

The End